Terry Perkins
and his
upside down frown

By Felix Massie

This is Terry Perkins.

Actually, no, wait...

This is Terry Perkins.

You see...

Around about the age that kids start standing on their feet
is around about the age that Terry Perkins tried to speak.

Terry's came out rather strange...
It made him rather sad.

Terry's puzzled mother
was really quite concerned,
and asked the doctor anxiously,
"Can his words be turned?"

like roll him down the stairs.

Terry liked to daydream that he lived in outer space: no upside down or sideways... It was the perfect place!

He thought for several minutes,
scratched his chin and said,
"Turn this strange boy upside down,
and place him on his head."

And so she did.

When Terry opened up his mouth,
some upright words came out!

The doctor smiled, his job was done.
"That's cured the boy, no doubt!"

So, it took him quite some time...
it took a little while...
but it seemed that Terry's frown
had turned into a smile.

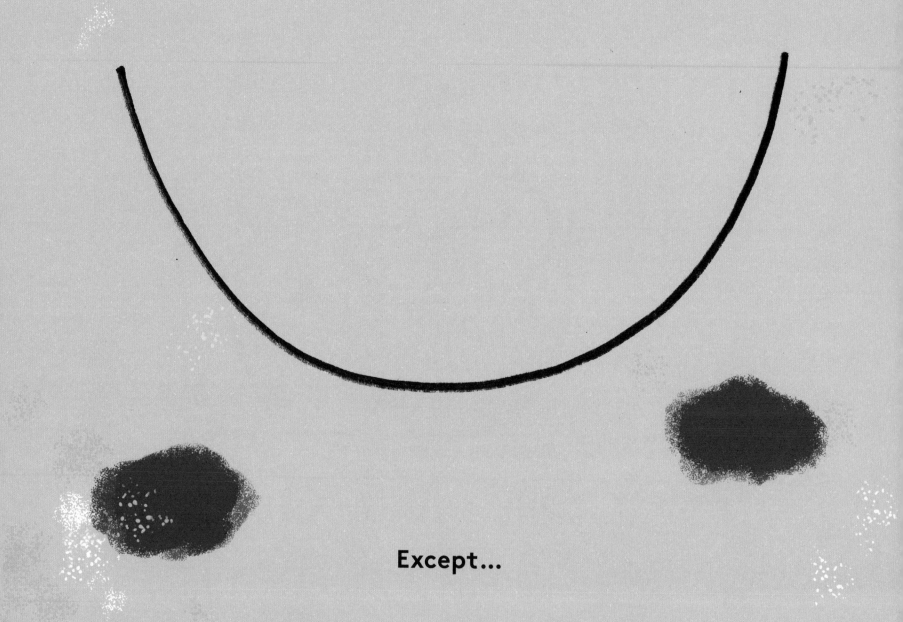

Except...

It was not a happy smile,
it was very much a frown.

Now when people looked at him,
his frown was upside down.

And Terry kept on frowning,
even though he could now talk:
upside down, stuck on his head,
now he couldn't walk!

Kids at playschool laughed at him,
for kids can be unfair.
They'd do some really horrid things,

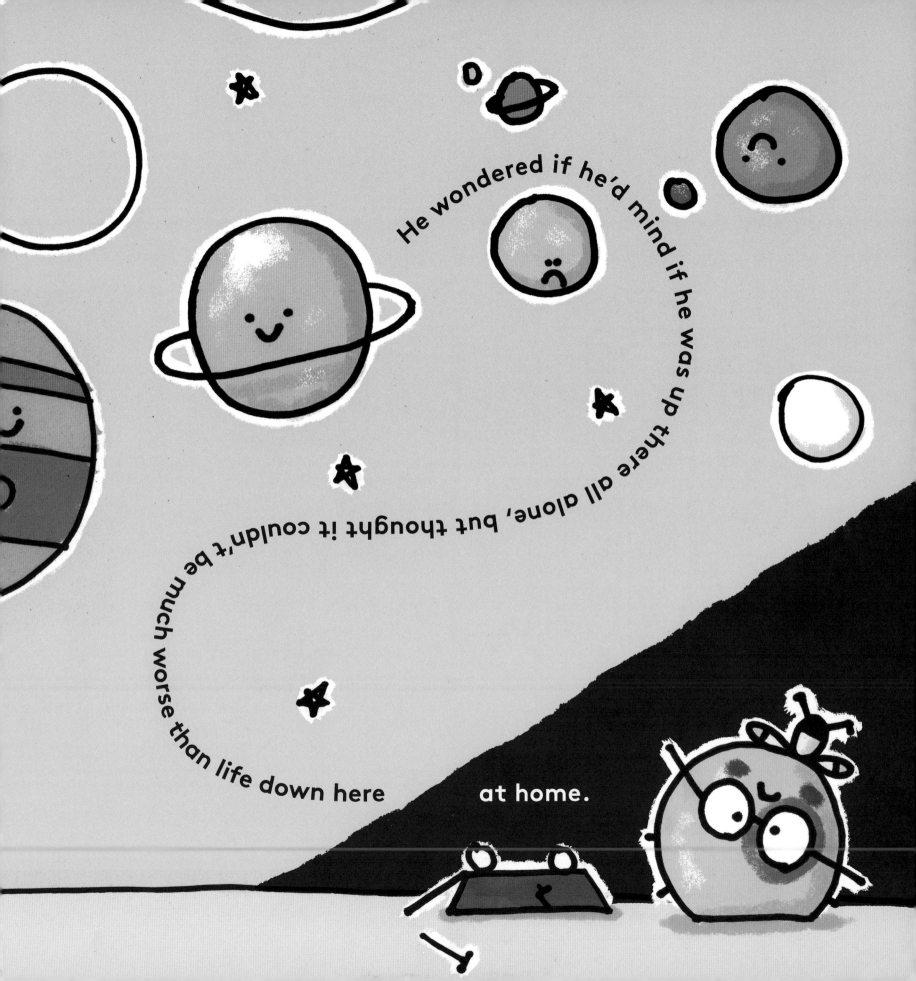

He wondered if he'd mind if he was up there all alone, but thought it couldn't be much worse than life down here

at home.

When he bumped back down to Earth,
he ran off to the park,
where he thought he'd be alone,
and stay till it got dark.

But he wasn't alone...

Jenny, on the monkey bars,
knew Terry from playschool.

She didn't think
that he was weird –
she thought he was quite cool!

She swung round quickly upside down
and meant to shout out...

boo!

But got her b's and p's confused
and loudly shouted...

Terry then did something that he
hadn't done before.
He found that he was rolling round
and laughing on the floor.

To Jenny, upside down-ness wasn't
stupid, strange or dumb.
She turned round Terry's point of view,
and showed him it was fun!

Together they would

roll,

and hang,

and jump,

and hop,

and flop,

and only when they wore out
would they ever think to stop.

So, sometimes it can take no time,
other times, a while,
but even an enormous frown
can turn into a smile.

You never need a reason
to stand up proud and tall:
being upside down or different
doesn't matter... at all!

The end

for Pam.

Text and illustrations copyright © Felix Massie 2015

The right of Felix Massie to be identified as the author and illustrator
of this work has been asserted by him in accordance with the Copyright,
Designs and Patents Act, 1988 (United Kingdom).

First published in hardback in Great Britain in 2015 by Frances Lincoln Children's Books.
First published in paperback in 2016 by Frances Lincoln Children's Books,
74-77 White Lion Street, London N1 9PF
www.franceslincoln.com

A catalogue record for this book is available from the British Library.

ISBN 978-1-84780-621-5

Illustrated digitally
Designed by Andrew Watson • Edited by Jenny Broom

Printed in China
1 3 5 7 9 8 6 4 2